TRACKED

Kadance Royal

ROYAL MEDIA
& PUBLISHING

Royal Media & Publishing
Jeffersonville, IN 47131
http://www.royalmediaandpublishing.com
royalmediapublishing@gmail.com

© Copyright – 2025

ISBN: 978-1-955501-29-3

Printed in the United States of America

Dedication

To every child that has gone missing, kidnapped or killed.

To every parent that has lost a child.

Acknowledgements

I thank my Lord and Savior Jesus Christ for giving me another opportunity to introduce more people to you. I thank you for entrusting this gift to me. Lord, let your Spirit move, guide and empower through this book to the people who will read it.

To my husband, Brian K. Royston, the love of my life, for loving and cheering me on so much that I can be and do all that God has placed in me. I love you.

To my mom, my greatest supporter and best friend. To my dad, who is in Heaven, who I know is proud of me and always encouraged me to go for it. Thanks to all the rest of my family for their love and support.

A special thank you to Rev. and Mrs. Claude R. Royston for their love and support.

To the rest of my clients, friends and family, thank you and love you always.

#Kadance

Table of Contents

Introduction

The contents in this book were very difficult to write. When I write fiction, I normally write positive, motivational and stories with a message that is happy or seeks to encourage or empower. I struggled to write books on grief for children which I asked God specifically to give me.

The basis for this book is a follow-up to the series "The Men of Roberts Junction." This series is told with male main characters, by a female author, but an action thriller and only alludes to the danger, corruption, family dysfunction and betrayal that occurred with the main characters, Hank, Duane and Xavier. But in the book 'Duane', his love interest discovers a way to put tracking devices inside jewelry. In the book 'Xavier', Xavier discovers that his family has been running not only a lucrative farm, but also a main transportation stop or spot on the "Human Railroad." I knew that "Tracked" was an idea for an extension of the Men of Roberts Junction series but the nature of the subject was not something I wanted to delve into. Why? It is too brutal and criminal to imagine let alone write about. I take writing very personally. All of my emotions, visual capabilities and senses are normally involved in my writing. I can see, taste, touch, smell and hear the people, characters and sounds of what is happening in the stories. My prayer has been that God only gives me the words, sounds, etc. in the daytime. I can't write any part of this book after 4:00 p.m. Why? I won't be able to sleep. I will be haunted by this tale. At this writing, I was awakened at 3:00 a.m. to start writing. I have an early appointment so I will be able to get at least 3 hours of writing in. Because I type 80+ words per minute, I wanted to get some of the most difficult scenes and chapters out of the way so that I would be assured to finish this novella prior to my personal deadline. I am my own publisher and have a deadline, due date and target to be finished that I placed on myself.

I must give a special shout out to Rev. Peggy B. Dixon who is the lead and true motivation to get this book done. She told me the subject matter and I opened my big mouth and told her my plan for the next book, "Tracked." So here we are.

For my own protection, I provided the very basics, alluded to some of the graphic content, but tried to stay away from the brutal, explicit details for my own mental health. What is in this book is only the tip of the iceberg. You can only imagine the depth, height and cruelty that goes into this type of operation and lifestyle. The evil, wickedness and little regard for human life that must be taken on to even participate on any level with this type of operation. This book is fiction and all of the characters. The town of Linkett doesn't exist in Kentucky and all of the activities are all fiction. Parts of the story are set in Lexington and the fictional Linkett and not Roberts Junction. The Lexington area is where Xavier is from and one of the primary targets or transitional locations for human trafficking in the story. There is farm land and very agricultural for transport. Any other resemblance to actual occurrences is on God.

My prayer is that this helps save someone's life. My prayer is that this in some way makes you teach your children even more about their own surroundings, safety and protection, hold them a little closer and love them even more.

Finally, let me be totally transparent with you about how much research I did on this topic. Little to none. I like sleeping at night and didn't want to spend months trying to shake off any spiritual or emotional attacks while writing the book. I realize that some things come with the territory, but I am not going to throw gasoline on this fire. This was written in obedience to God. It's not meant to be a reflection or attack on any given town or city but the horrible activity as a whole. Of course, as an author, the goal is to get these words and voices out of my head that clearly want me to tell this story. I am thrilled to revisit the "Men of Roberts Junction" now married to the women that they love, but this journey is not filled with romantic, fun, and sexy banter, This gives you just a small insight into real life evil, criminology, manipulation and death. Not a subject that I would pick to write about, but it picked me.

The Confirmation

Finally, finally I was dropping off a book order to a client. I rarely do this because I normally just ship the books to them directly, but was led to deliver them to the client. I followed God's instructions. When I was leaving the house of the client and near my car, 3 children, upper elementary age between 3rd and 5th grade were crossing the street and they spoke to me first and then I spoke back and asked them about school. They told me their school but were also excited to tell me, a stranger, that someone in some restaurant somewhere as they were walking home was offering them ice cream. They were complaining because they didn't get the ice cream because they needed $8.00. They didn't have the money and all 3 of them were disappointed. I told my husband the story and he thought I gave them the $8.00 but I was not led to give them anything. But was very disappointed as well to know that they trusted someone to tell her that story on a street that was isolated, they were alone and I was standing right next to a car. What if I had been the wrong type of person? What if I had someone around the corner to signal a white van to take them to get some ice cream or ask them for a favor to get the $8.00? You see where I am going with this tale. Adding to this very sad tale is the fact that this happened recently. Not back in the 1970's or 1980's, but in the year of our Lord, 2025. What a sad commentary. None of the three of them were even concerned that maybe they didn't need to get the ice cream from the restaurant and/or should not even have spoken to any adult besides hello near that restaurant stopping long enough for the offer of ice cream or the fact that they needed to be safe and watch out for each other and be careful around adults in the first place. They just wanted ice cream.

This was confirmation that I wasn't going to get away with not writing this novella. I asked God if the previous series would be enough and He said, "No. Someone has to tell this story." I guess it is me.

Let's go!

Kadance/Julia

Home

"Welcome to Monday Day Break on WLIN news, right here in Linkett, Kentucky I'm River Waters. The latest statistics from the United Nations' International Labor Organization states that 27.6 million people are victimized and 77% of the victims are for forced labor and 23% are for sex trafficking. In an effort to combat the ever-increasing human trafficking problem, there is a new technology discovery that allows a tracking chip to be placed in jewelry that a person would wear and hopefully, within the first 24 hours, the person would be found and returned home to their family. The inventor would like to remain anonymous but hopes that their efforts along with collaboration with many non-profit organizations, these devices which look like very stylish jewelry can be used to save lives. Now in other news..."

Larisa Tate pushed the remote control to turn off the tv as quickly as that short snippet of the story ended. "We will never catch these crooks and stop it for good as long as the media keeps tipping them off!" she said out loud in her condo as she threw the remote to the other side of her couch.

In spite of all of the crime, Larisa Tate was still proud of her city, Linkett, Kentucky. Filled with horse farms, horse racing, blue grass and basketball. The big green machine is a whole vibe, tribe, and multi-million-dollar business. The people in the area are primarily put into three categories, filthy rich, work hard to raise a family, pay rent and have some quality of life or be bottom poor. No matter what category you are in, as an alum and graduate, when the sports season comes around, whether you are sitting on the floor or in the highest top seat, people will find a way and money to see their team. It's an escape from whatever life that they normally live when they walk through the doors of the Arena during basketball season or the Football Stadium. The playing field is leveled and we are all seeing the same game at the same time no matter whether you walked, drove or caught the bus to get there.

Amazingly enough on the other side of life, Linkett University has an endowment worth millions that they struggle to find students to give scholarships to every year because they won't cross the street, go up the hill, register, qualify, go to class, take the exams, pass them all and get a degree. They would rather live a life below their privilege. They would rather sleep around, get government assistance, hustle their way to jail or even more so, die poor than live a different life. It takes guts to succeed. It takes guts to walk away from what you know, what you've been taught and how you were raised to live a different life. The name

Linkett had been used in many promotional campaigns for people to connect, collaborate and collectively progress to a better life. The connections were designed for good but evil always seemed to rear its ugly head.

Larisa Tate was from Linkett but always wanted more. She was the oldest and named after a perfect blend of both of her parents, Larry and Lisa Tate.

The shotgun house that she grew up in which was small, narrow, has a small living room, two small bedrooms with an even smaller bathroom and the kitchen is somehow in the back of the house with a backdoor that leads to an even smaller backyard. It was always clean and even spotless some would say. The rent to own furniture was now the Tates which took years to pay off given their small salaries, but they always put their money together and fought to love each other and stay together no matter what. Larisa knew all of her neighbors, and they knew her. She knew which kids she could play with and which kids she couldn't go near, talk to, let alone, even play in their front yard. Her parents taught her well even though they didn't go to college. They married young and just worked hard. Linkett was home for them. Third generation Linkett natives. What else is there? Where would they go? Everything they knew was right here in Linkett. Some things they really didn't need to know or even want to know but would soon know more than they ever knew existed right here in Linkett, KY.

Larisa was pretty and always looked much younger than her actual age. She was actually 25 but could easily pass for 16. She, along with her brother and sister, had goals and dreams which were surprisingly instilled in them by their parents.

Their parents always encouraged them to go across the street, Vine Street to college. Larisa studied forensic science and criminology and joined the Linkett police force. Her brother, Larry, Jr. was a lawyer and his parents were so proud because he had previously graduated cum laude with a degree in political science and works in one of the largest law firms in their town. Their youngest sister, Leena was a doctor and general practitioner in a multi-doctor office in town. The Tates were so proud of their children and the next generation of Tates that they could bust. They told everyone that would listen, all about the accomplishments of their children. Until they couldn't tell anyone anymore about their children's lives. Why? The Tate children were now seeing things and living lives that they couldn't even tell their parents about.

Linkett High School

Monday morning, school was in session as normal. The students were buzzing through the hallways, complaining, preparing, teasing each other but a small group of girls always held the attention of the boys nearby.

Saundra, Melanie and Cindy were three "kind of" friends since kindergarten standing in the hallway. Kind of friends because Saundra Watson was the leader. She always had been the leader and always will be the leader of the group if you remained in the group. Whatever she said, the other two were supposed to do, no questions asked. Why would you not want to be friends with Saundra? She was the head cheerleader, President of almost all of the best clubs in the building and her dad was an important special police officer of some kind. Melanie and Cindy asked about it once, but it was so secretive that Saundra said that she couldn't talk about it. What teenager doesn't want to be in the "in crowd" at any high school? Friends, popularity, and notoriety are the three essentials to surviving the teenage years and beyond. You get to be put in the front of the line, get the best seats and access to all of the insider information, jokes and parties. A teenager's dream came true or was it a nightmare?

"Hey want to link up? We're in Linkett after all," Bo Rice said as he passed these very popular three girls in the hallway at Linkett High School. Bo had only been at Linkett for three years, tall, handsome with a full beard even though he was still in high school. He always knew who the important and influential students were in a school.

Melanie giggled. She was the smart but not so attractive girl of the group. Slightly thick but not too thick to be categorized as fat. Melanie secretly loved Bo but knew that he was way out of her league. Saundra rolled her eyes. She was clearly the beauty queen and the school said so by voting her the homecoming queen for the past two years. Saundra replied, "Don't you have anything better to say?"

"Nope, I just wanted to see you roll your eyes just once today at me," Bo replied with a smile. He was not athletic enough for the varsity team but the community basketball teams always picked him.

"High school boys are just so stupid acting and always saying stupid stuff like that. Why don't you grow up?" Saundra asked.

"Why, am I not a teenager? I should say stupid stuff like that to girls like you. Don't hate the player who is trying to shoot his shot. You must still be on one of those dating apps, acting like you are 25 when you know that you are just 15," Bo said.

"Ugh, you get on my nerves," Saundra rolled her eyes again.

"Two times in one conversation you have rolled your eyes at me. This has made my whole week, let alone my day," Bo said as he walked off.

Melanie thought, 'I wish he would look at me like that.

Cindy said nothing. She had learned that her silence was her coping mechanism. It was one way to keep her from being noticed and possibly bullied but she wasn't blind. Cindy watched the whole conversation and exchange. She knew that Bo was up to no good and so was Saundra.

"Let's get to class before the bell rings," Saundra said as she closed her locker and headed toward class but stopped suddenly and said, "Cindy with your quiet ass. If you told anybody about what I do outside of this school, you will NOT be hanging out with me anymore and your cool card will be revoked. You ain't got to say nothing because I know that you heard me."

Cindy heard Saundra alright. She still said nothing and didn't drop her head because she knew it would give her away. She loved hanging out with Saundra. To be the cool kid once in her life was awesome. She had a horrible home life, an abusive stepfather and a mother who would not or could not stand up for herself let alone her children. Cindy felt like she was out in the world all by herself with no help, protection or hopeful outlook on life. What would happen to her? What kind of future would she have coming from a little small, in the middle of nowhere town like Linkett in a state known for basketball, horse racing, bourbon and a whole lot of sin?

Cindy knew that she and Melanie were just along for the ride. Melanie at least had a stable home life and parents who at least acted like they cared about her. Melanie rolled her eyes when she ever talked about her parents and their 'goofy' ways but Cindy wished she had someone to show her the 'goofy' kind of love or attention. She spent most of her home time, in her room, hiding with her headphones on to drown out the noise.

Later that evening, Saundra was home alone again. No parents were in the house. Mom was out with friends partying and Dad was always working. Saundra always wondered why they even had her? They didn't even like her, spend time with her but just a photo op for the holidays or to show her off when important people came to town during the racing season at the Derby or Keeneland. She wasn't a priority to her parents so with time on her hands she decided to gain the attention of someone who had made her a priority.

She logged in to a dating app. She saw that 'he' went live shortly after she did.

School had taught students long ago that you never know who is logging in, man or woman, friend or foe on dating apps. They warned to be careful, never meet them period but especially, don't meet anyone alone. People online are anonymous for a reason. But did Saundra listen? No. The abuse of neglect was why she logged in every day.

That familiar handle, 'realman22' logged in shortly after Saundra did.

"Hey beautiful what's up?"

"Nothing, just relaxing"

"Well, what if I came over and relaxed with you?"

"Nope, can't do that. I don't have my own place. I have roommates."

"Well, I could bring over some roommates to keep them company while I keep you company."

"Nope, we stay strictly online. Nothing else."

"Why? You're hurting my heart."

"Sorry."

"Don't be sorry, make me happy."

"Are you happy? What about me being happy?"

"I can do that too."

"Really?"

"Really. You need a real man. That's the reason for my handle, 'realman22' I am a real man. Stop playing with them little boys and get you a real man."

No reply. Saundra knew that this was wrong. She knew that she was only 16 and she didn't know this guy for real but he was so nice online. He talked to her so nicely. Complimented her in every conversation no matter what her day was like. Her parents didn't understand her.

They spent so much time working, partying with their friends, golfing and at the club. They left her alone and really didn't care what she did. They were just happy when they logged into the parent portal to see her good grades, awards on the school website and she had enough balance on her personal credit card to keep her out of their hair. No abuse, no harsh words, just years of neglect and being raised by babysitting services or nannies. Who would pay attention to her? Who would show her the affection and positivity that she so desperately wanted and needed? Would her need to override common sense prevail? Only time would tell.

"Sorry about that. I didn't mean to come off so hard at you about being a real man but you are so pretty from your profile picture that I just wanted you to know how much I am here for you. I'm concerned and care about you so much just talking to you online. Are you still there?"

The conversation ended.

"Damn," realman22 said under his breath.

"Will is she gone?" Bo asked.

"Gone," Will said, "I guess I came on too strong,"

"You always do but she'll be back. You know how pretty girls are. I'll check the temperature at school tomorrow. She acts like she hates me but, I know that they love the attention and compliments."

"True and the revenge trap is almost set," Will replied.

The Problem

On that same Monday morning, 40 miles away, Larisa was headed into the office. Larisa knew that trouble was brewing. After full body scans, eye scans and a badge review, she entered the secret underground headquarters. On the street level floor, it looked like any other office building but once you gained access through and past security, you entered a totally different world on a very secretive lower level of the building.

After 5 years on the force, Larisa was recruited and trained for a special forces' operation for human trafficking. Because she was from Linkett, a mix of small town, farm town and so close to a much bigger city, it had become a major stop, transport and sorting station after kidnapping of children or adults took place. Lexington still had the traits of being a college and an agricultural dynasty but with the money to fund whatever activities could go on whether legal or criminal within any distance local or global. Larisa, although based in Lexington, worked closely with the Linkett force and locals there to give them the specific traits, movements, and suspects for the 'human railroad.' She knew that the small town of Linkett didn't have the money or job opportunities that were in nearby Lexington and thus, the opportunity to be influenced by illegal money was great. She also notified her siblings of the potential hazards since they were still actually located in Linkett. Larry, Jr. was now in a law office that provided general legal advice so that was corporate to criminal cases. Leena was a nurse practitioner in a group practice. By all standards, they were each successful but their jobs never superseded their love and support for their family.

They would meet secretly away from their parents in an old barn on their family property about 10 miles away from Linkett. Her parents refused to work the land but kept it in the family. The only building still left of the original buildings was the barn. The house had since been torn down, the livestock was sold years ago and the small family cemetery remained to remind them always of their history. Larisa and her siblings restored the barn for their own personal reasons. Although on special assignment, she could get home in less than an hour.

The human railroad had many stops, customers, and pieces of the puzzle to make it move. It was always known that the real 'engine' to make the railroad move was power, politics and money. These are people with power and money with abnormal sexual appetites and demented desires for control and abuse on others. The railroad always seemed to be able to recruit, extort and bribe, friend or foe, lie or truth, in one way shape or form to convince others to be the driving force to keep the engine moving. One captured person said, "It's a horrible job but they made me do it."

Today, like always, Larisa laid down her personal items on her desk. She was always careful with her every move because she knew that she was always being watched. Not just by the cameras in the building but seemingly, her biggest rival for the Commander Watson's attention, William Rice. William Rice was her desk mate and located so close that she always felt like she had to hide her computer screen, purse and phone from his eyes. He could show up out of no where and at any time.

"Good morning, Larisa," William Rice.

"William," was all of the response and attention that Larisa was willing to give him. He somehow had become the thorn in her side and her competitor for what they were competing for she didn't know.

Suddenly, Larisa could hear Commander Watson, as well as everyone outside of his office literally yelling, "I'm doing all that you say and working as hard as I can! Give me a break!" Commander Watson had been a police officer for 20 years and for the past five years, was assigned the lead agent position to the special task force on human trafficking. It was a very stressful job, high profile job that kept him away from home most evenings because he was busy networking and involved in much politics in the city, state and region.

He pressed send on the cell phone and literally threw it across his office in anger and disgust.

William ran to his door and asked, "Commander what's going on? I can see that you are troubled and I'm ready to help,"

"Get out William! Larisa come in here!"

Larisa spun her chair quickly and headed into his office.

"Close the door!" Commander yelled again and turned so that his back was to Larisa.

She didn't sit down in the chair at his desk but stood instead because she didn't quite know what was coming next.

"I can see that and we all heard it. What's going on?" Larisa asked while taking a quick look down at his desk. Files, papers and pictures were everywhere and in no order that she could see but, a messy and unorthodox system of his.

"The railroad is moving and carrying a lot of property," Commander Watson said as he turned back around and plopped down in his chair.

Larisa knew exactly what that meant. There had been a rise in kidnappings, child, male or female and abducted by any means necessary.

"Linkett?" Larisa asked.

"Linkett," Commander said.

"I saw the news this morning exposing the jewelry tracking which is not helping our case any,"

"Yes and I'm wondering what will possibly be invented next for human safety. Have you heard anything Larisa?"

"No, why would I have heard anything? You're the lead on this case and tell us what to do," Larisa inquired.

"Well, I know that you have a brother and sister who are working in Linkett and thought they might have told you something that they have seen or heard,"

"I keep my personal life and work life separate. I wouldn't want to put my family in any danger from this job. Given the case that we are currently working on, it just too much to risk. These people are ruthless and killers. So, what's next to possibly stop them?" Larisa asked calmly but a huge alarm went off in her head. The statement went past anything she had ever heard Commander ask her before. Had he been compromised or working on both sides of this case?

"First off, all ports and borders are on high alert. The Ohio River is on very high alert because we have found out that the barges are moving more than coal from Eastern Kentucky. Every mode of transportation is being used to get property outside of the borders overseas. The price is higher overseas although the property is paid a hefty price inside the U.S.," Commander said.

"It's so terrible all of the lives that are traumatized by these movers," Larisa said.

"Exactly but you know this goes pretty high up," Commander said.

"I know," Larisa said with sadness. She had seen the pictures, the reports of the murders and realized that undercover was not for her but her strength was to be the support team, the eyes, ears and resources. Inside the operation, and undercover, she didn't have the mental or physical fortitude for it. She had also seen the agents that had been under and come out. They were never the same.

"There is a team coming soon. The goal is to coordinate our efforts and you may have to direct them. They know old Linkett and not new Linkett," Commander said as he came from behind his desk and sat down closer to Larisa.

"Sure, I'll do what I can but where is all of this property going?" Larisa asked.

"Several places and then overseas,"

"How are you so sure?"

"You know we have our sources,"

"I'm sure,"

"At this point, you will be the eyes, ears, background, reference for this operation. You could never go undercover in this area, it would never work,"

"I understand," Larisa said and she knew everyone person on his desk from her very quick peek. Her photogenic brain had always worked in her favor.

"Agents are in place and working to find out as much information as possible. In the meantime, before we put them directly in harm's way, we have to secure their safety to get in as well as get back out. If they are discovered, they are terminated permanently and you know what I mean. They always send back a horrible and gruesome message to police that we don't try it again. But there are other innocent lives at stake,"

"In our city, state and outside our borders of course,"

"Never to be seen or heard of again. Case cold and closed. You know we don't have many friends overseas as it is,"

"I understand," Larisa replied. Deep down she knew that they had to do all that they could but these cases were always so disheartening because even if someone in the organization or on the 'train' as it was sometimes called, was captured, others would take their place. The money was too great in spite of the horrific tasks. They could get close but road blocks always stopped them from making any great arrests or convictions.

On her burner phone which was silent but the notification came to Larisa's watch was a text from her sister, Leena. It was a group text, that only they saw. The phones were not traccable but they could never be too cautious. They had themselves to protect as well as their parents. Criminals always go after what you love, to force you to do things that you hate.

She looked down at her watch.

The text read, 'meet at the spot.'

"What's up Dick Tracy?" Commander asked while watching her look at her watch.

"Oh wow, listen at you. Nothing just family stuff. It's amazing how technology has caught up to the sci-fi shows,"

"You're too young for Dick Tracy," Commander said.

"Tell that to my dad,"

They both laughed and Larisa replied to the text. Larisa sat at her desk reviewing files and information that had already been gathered to prepare for the upcoming meetings. She also made a list of the people that she saw on Commander's desk. It took her down memory lane to see among those images, her best friend from high school, Normalinda Martin and the guy who got away, Alexander Drew Harris.

One of many of the unfortunate things about this job was that she didn't know who to trust. It was so complex and deceitful that she kept all relationships on a surface level.

The most important people whom she knew that she could trust were her siblings. Their meeting later this evening was where she could be safe and as transparent as possible for their protection as well. She would find out what they knew about later.

On Monday evening in Linkett at the Tates' house.

"It looks like the kids are here," Larry, Sr. said as he came in from the hardware store for dinner, "Their cars are here, but they're taking the ATVs."

"LT, you know where their spot is," Lisa said.

"I wonder what they talk about out there," Larry, Sr. pondered.

"Leave them alone, LT. Let them meet in private. I've been warned by Larisa that whatever they're talking about, they only need to be talking about it with the three of them. They're trying to protect us, save us from any heartache. They know what they're doing,"

"I know Lisa that they are all grown up but they will never be that grown up. They are still our babies," LT said quickly.

"Always will be but they're not little babies but grown babies. They got grown people bills, grown people problems but my gut tells me that there is a bigger grown-up problem that has to do with their jobs and not us so again, leave them alone I tell you, Lisa insisted.

"I wish I knew but at least we raised them to have each other," LT replied.

"That's a blessing,"

"I still wish I knew,"

"Nope, you don't want to know,"

"You know and won't tell me,"

"No that's not it because they wouldn't tell me either. But a mother always knows that it's serious and important. So, it's best that we both stay right here and don't go out there. Sit your behind in your comfy chair. Watch your favorite program. Watch a little bit of the news. When they come from their meeting, they'll come in the house to say goodbye before they leave," Lisa said.

"All right," LT gave in as he stomped just a little bit harder as he sat down in his chair.

"Larry, it's going to be okay,"

"Um," was all he could say.

Meanwhile, in their spot in the barn, is where the Tate children met. They had built a lower level under the barn complete with security, seclusion and safety for just in case. They divided the expense three ways, only had construction done enough to make it look like a family room or man cave and the other parts they had to hire very covert operatives to put in the remaining security systems piece by piece and separately. Once they get to the barn, they drive directly inside and close the door behind them and ride an elevator down to the lower level. They can use short wave walkie talkies to communicate. Even the burner phones or anything else that can be traced, are left turned off and in their cars.

They committed to confiding in each other, any information they knew. And if anything leaks, they know where it came from, one of the three of them. Video cameras are everywhere. Larry, Jr. may be a lawyer but he was raised by his dad as a handy man.

Once they are seated, Larisa starts, "This is what I know so far. Property has started being acquired and they are getting ready to start moving. On the legal side, LJ I don't know what's gonna come up. Leena, on the medical side you need to be on the lookout."

"You're late, they have already started,"

"Already?"

"Yep, I know that when property is acquired, they start reviewing and evaluating it. Assessing it. Get blood work done, tagging and sorting the property,"

"I really don't like it that we know the terminology,"

"I hate it too, but better to know than to not know and be left in the dark," Leena said.

"I guess we can never go back to the dark, can we Risa?" LJ added.

"Nope,"

"I noticed it already. It's the doctor's office next to ours. They're not running in our office. But when I came outside to head to my car to go to lunch, I saw like six ambulances with two stretchers each in them. Some had small kids, some had teenagers in them. They were moving them in two by two really quickly. I asked when I came back from lunch, what's going on over there, next door? They were like, nothing, you don't need to know,"

"Who said that you don't need to know?"

"The receptionist,"

"Where's their name?"

"I'll give it to you. I'm suspecting that the office where I am knows what's going on next door and being paid not to say. I didn't inquire any further because I knew we would be meeting and I wanted you to know what I had seen already. That's the reason why I called the meeting. And so, I figured. That property had started being moved.

Yeah, that's the cleansing process, that's the evaluation and review process where they take off all of their jewelry, take their clothes off, start examining, tagging them, where, which way they're supposed to go, etc. Most of them are not awake. While they are doing the cleansing process, they are asleep with those new sleep patches. So that they won't wake up and cause a lot of disturbance in the scene,"

"What about going to the bathroom and stuff?" LJ asked.

"Catheters,"

"Wow,"

"After reviewing is the breaking process before you're headed to Distribution,"

"Yuck,"

"You can say that again. The babies aren't normally broken, because they are too young to know the difference. They'll just be trained for new parents or owners. Others are broken in house before distribution and others are broken, groomed and trained once they are distributed."

"Why can't we seem to get them tracked and returned before all of this process happens?" LJ asked.

"Someone found out about the tracking jewelry and that's the reason why all of the jewelry is removed. It was even announced on the news! On the legal side, we're always trying to find out the next link and the locals are so dirty that they never, ever seem to get the search warrants in a timely fashion that we need to catch them red handed, legally or in the act. Without the warrants, we can't search and then they are long gone,"

"This is the most horrible thing I can ever think of. I cannot imagine having my baby, child, girlfriend or wife missing and gone. No body to claim, no answers to the questions, just bye. Nothing can ever be done about it. A mystery goes forever unsolved."

"Well, I know I didn't call the meeting Leena did but I overheard two people in a conference room saying that there'll soon be an Amber Alert for a daughter missing to someone high up in the area. It's somehow related to a political client," LJ said.

"Where were you?" Larisa said.

"In the supply closet that is off from the conference room and the copy room getting supplies. They didn't see me but I definitely heard them. I went out through the copy room so they would not suspect,"

"Great job. Was the door opened or closed?"

"Open slightly. Why?"

"They meant for somebody to hear. Are there cameras in the office?"

"Everywhere,"

"They know that you heard them and if something is said or told then they'll know it was you that told. Did you know the voices?"

"Yeah and I'll let you know. I left before the specifics just heard just that much. I have also just seen people in the waiting room but my gut tells me that they're dirty. I just know it. I also can't stand it that the firm is willing to take them on," LJ said.

"Say nothing, remember this goes really high and goes really deep. That also means that I can't say anything even in the office until after the Amber alert comes out," Larisa said.

"Don't worry about me. I wasn't supposed to hear what I did hear already," LJ said.

"Back to the doctor's office in the area with all of those ambulances? Can't you raid it?" Leena asked.

"We've raided that building so many times it's not funny. Wherever they have their bodies, it's not in the main office," Larisa.

"I think they take them underground. They built another office underneath. But it's secret and it's locked, so you just can't roll up in there and see the bodies in there. They take them on to another level," Leena thinks.

"We're dealing with people with deep pockets and accomplices in really high places, senators, governors, all the way up," Larisa said.

"I don't know whether I need to stay on with this firm or strike out on my own?" LJ asked.

"As horrible as it is, you need to stay and you need to know about everything. Hopefully you won't ever have to work on any of the cases but, at least you know who some of the players are and actually what they do," Larisa said.

"With that said, big Sister, how are we going to protect our parents?" Leena asked.

"I hope mom can keep Dad in the house, occupied. And not come out here and try to overhear anything we're talking about," LJ said.

"Good luck with that," Leena replied.

"Well, it's been okay so far, Mom is very convincing," Larisa added.

"Dad is really nosey when it comes to us," LJ said.

"Yeah," Leena said.

"We'll see. Protecting them is of utmost importance but giving them the codes to get underground is a last resort. Understand?"

"Last resort but what's the sign to pull the trigger and get them underground?"

"I don't know yet but Trigger is the code word. Got it. Trigger is the code word."

"Got it but what's next?" LJ asked.

"Commander says that we've got a team coming in with more information and agents who are undercover already, but this is still a major stop for the 606 train," Larisa said.

"So, the objective is to keep the property here, catch them before they leave the 606, right?"

"Right but the legal command is so slow that the window for the property to move is usually too late and they are gone before warrants can be issued,"

"So, what happens if we can't stop them from moving and the property leaves from the 606 areas?" LJ asked.

"Hopefully, they can be tracked before they get to the ports, but once they get to ports and get on boats, it's hard to get them back. Especially back into the area where they belong. The news actually reported the tracking jewelry that Annette Wilson made. They've tipped off the kidnappers and with the jewelry removed, there is no tracking device," Larisa said.

"I saw that too and thought about Annette. How do you get WLIN news Risa?"

"I subscribe. I have to keep tabs on you guys here," Larisa said.

They all chuckled.

"But back to the movement, it's gotten so bad that they are moving property in plain sight. They used to do it all at night," Larisa said.

"It all stinks as far as I'm concerned," Leena said.

"Yeah, but the players keep changing. They rotate out people and the insiders who are slowing down the legal side keep changing as well. It goes so high, there's so many people, it's hard for us to even keep track of it. Not to mention who might be dirty on the inside. Lincoln had that dirty cop ring not long ago and it took years to find out and break it down. Who knows? Even inside headquarters there may be somebody tipping them off. Everybody has a price. Linkett is so small that's the reason why they've done a lot of work here because they know who the players, movers and shakers are but we don't. Since there's not a lot of jobs in the area, people are willing to get money whether it's legal or illegal to survive,"

"Yuck," Leena muttered.

"Anything else we all need to know?" Larisa asked.

Leena and LJ just shook their heads no.

"Now keep your hands clean. Keep your ears and eyes open. Don't use burner phones unless we just have to. We don't communicate anything that we have discussed. That's it. If we have anything else to say, we always use code. Remember going to the movies? Let's have dinner. Not even meet at mom and dad's house. Going to the movies. How are you doing, man? Taking a shower. Text me later. Any questions?" Larisa asked.

"Nope this is a lot already," LJ replied.

"Let's go in the house, have dinner and try to be normal while we enjoy our parents. I love you both," Larisa said and they got on their ATVs, excited and locked the barn down.

In Plain Sight

Monday night at 9:00 p.m., long after most kids should be in bed, at the Linkett private country club a meeting was about to be held. Now Linkett and its country club may be small but it works for the community as a prestigious meeting spot for members only. The meeting looked like most business meetings, but the participants arrived in luxury cars, dressed well, expensive jewelry and tipped every serving staff very well. The tips to the serving staff were that they wouldn't talk. Their cars were all positioned and parked in the front door but they entered the building through a side entrance. There were cameras in the front entrance but the First Conductor had paid to turn off the cameras in the side entrance.

Steak, Lobster, Racks of Lamb and every side dish they desired was served during the late-night meeting. Early mornings were out of the question because that was when the most people were in attendance. It was after the club closed that they entered.

The table was all set. The food came immediately as soon as they sat down and placed family style. Drinks were set on a separate bar in the room and then all staff left the room and never returned until the meeting ended. As normal, there was a text sent that they were done and they exited within 20 minutes and then the serving staff returned to the room to clean and clear it.

"Let's call this meeting to order Train 606," the First Conductor said, "Does everyone have their drink order?"

"Yeah, yes, you bet," everyone chimed in around the table.

"Great, we can get started. Property has already been acquired for the adoption centers, etc. These are easy acquisitions as parents are not watching or paying attention, especially the young parents and I use this term loosely. The primary purpose of our business today is that new older property needs to be acquired. The specifications are in the folders in front of you, your assignments and the quota is provided. Any questions?"

"Are all of the stations prepared for the new property?" one person asked.

"Yes, everyone has been alerted. Your job now is to scout out the property and then notify us when the property would best be acquired," the First Conductor said.

"Would a party be best?" another person asked.

"Party would be the easlest to acquire the YA property but risky because there would be so much of this property moving at the same time raising suspicion and making us vulnerable for an outcry and investigation from the community," the First Conductor said.

"Don't we have the inside operatives on mute enough and well paid to keep that from happening?" another asked.

"Yes, but there are always non-profit organizations sending in agents, officers and others to try to infiltrate Train 606 network and given the requests and requesters of this property and the profit being generated, we can't have this,"

"Agreed," everyone said around the table.

"So, a party is the easiest but it has to be invitation only. Only 5-10 invitations, then lay low and then start again. It can take up to 6 weeks for us to get the property that we need but it is possible and that is the easiest. The sleep stage will have to be longer but once that stage is over, then breaking and then transport.

Remember we can't get sloppy and not follow instructions so that we take care of our clients and not get infiltrated or caught. Understand?"

"Yes Boss," everyone said throughout the table.

"We leave at 11 and you've got 20 to get out and exit the premises. Any questions?" the First Conductor asked with one quick sweep around the room, "Well, let's eat and drink," the First Conductor said.

"Yeah!" they all agreed. Their own party began because they had much work to do. Everyone enjoyed the scrumptious food. Rocking to the music, laughing and teasing each other but this life was no laughing matter. They would be ruining lives, ignoring human cries and doing whatever it took for the almighty dollar.

They began planning their schemes, routes and movements throughout the city and region to acquire the much-needed requests from their clients. As much as this was a dehumanizing operation, it was business, for others they had been groomed for these positions and trapped by the money, and others had been desensitized by the humanness of life with little options but just survival.

The Second Conductor, just called "second", sat down next to the First Conductor and asked, "What's up with Alex?"

"I don't know but we must keep an eye on him. I saw the same thing,"

"He's not enjoying the food. Not planning his next move. We've got work to do but this is the fun before the work,"

"It's not right. I don't know if he has the guts, the 'know how', the stomach for this work or if he is about to go soft,"

"Exactly. I've got to get his folder again to figure out how he joined Train 606," First Conductor said.

"Right First," the Second Conductor said as he stood up and went back to his place at the other end of the table.

Alex was keen enough to know that something was brewing. He had been here long enough to know that it never was going to be a good thing when first and second were talking. Anybody else, it didn't matter. He kept his head down, talked little, kept eating and drinking.

Train 606 was the most advanced train in this most notorious network of this kind. There were multiple layers of contacts, pay offs, connections and people willing to keep Train 606 moving. The property must arrive at its destination in the best condition and to the customers satisfaction. No stone could be left unturned. No detail could be missed. There were no weak links that could be tolerated but just exterminated. There was always enough money to pay escape routes for those that couldn't stand up to the tasks at hand.

"Time's up and the party is over. You have 20 minutes," First Conductor said. Everyone knew what that meant. The work began. They took the last sips of their drinks; fist bumped the people around them and headed for the door. Alex headed toward the door as well but felt First Conductor and Second Conductor's eyes were on him.

All exited the building and the cars peeled off one by one in every direction in a horrific search of their next property. They worked most of the night planning, plotting and preparing for either night time acquisitions or day time with extreme calculations. The dark kept them under wraps and most of the time, the property was long gone, under lock and key hours before they knew that they were gone.

The following Tuesday at Linkett High School, Train 606 was on the move. The party was planned, prepared and the invitations were sent out. Mysteriously 10 invitations were strategically placed on the lockers of 5 females and 5 males at Linkett High School. The invitation was written to appear as a congratulations and you've been picked because they were in the 'elite' in-crowd. Cindy saw the envelope first and pointed it out to Saundra.

"What's this?" Cindy asked.

"I don't know but give it to me, it was on my locker door not yours," Saundra said as she grabbed the envelope, "An exclusive party! Yes! I love it. Invitation only."

"Where is this party?" Melanie asked.

"According to this envelope, I'm sworn to secrecy which makes it even more special."

"Well, at least when is it?" Melanie asked.

"Friday night at 9:00 p.m." Saundra said with a huge smile.

"That's late," Cindy said.

"Of course, that's when all of the great parties start, stupid." Saundra said as she rolled her eyes.

Cindy hated being called stupid or made to feel stupid. When would she ever learn how to get away from this girl and make some new friends? She decided to put herself on mute.

"I thought we were going to the game Friday?" Melanie reminded her.

"We are but you guys will stay at the game and I'll be headed to this address for food, fun and grownups," Saundra said.

"Does it allow for a plus one or two?" Melanie asked while looking at Cindy.

"If it did, I wouldn't take either of you because the envelope only had my name on it," Saundra said.

"That doesn't sound safe," Melanie muttered.

"I'll be safe with my mace, phone and beauty while you two will be safe at the game," Saundra said proudly.

"Okay if you say so but, I wouldn't go alone even if it was an invitation only party," Cindy encouraged.

"That's why you weren't invited and I was. Don't tell me what you would or wouldn't do because you are NOT me," Saundra filled with arrogance.

"Do you boo," Melanie said knowing that she couldn't change her mind.

"Yes, I'm going to do me," Saundra said emphatically.

Melanie and Cindy just looked at each other behind her back as they had for so many years knowing deep down inside that this was a huge mistake.

The Tracking Team

The next morning, Larisa arrived at headquarters in Lexington, they had company. A team of six people arrived, Hank and Jasmine Simpson, Duane and Annette Jackson along with Xavier and Normalinda Martin.

"Good morning to you all. I was just expecting the Jacksons, I didn't realize that they brought a team with them," Commander said, greeting them at the door loud enough for all to hear.

Larisa thought that was strange especially since Commander had already told her that a team was coming in the next few days. When did Commander start lying or did he just forget to keep up with his lies?

All six just looked at him in the face and nodded their heads and spoke no words.

The commander turned to the others in the room. "Can I have everyone's attention, please? We have visitors who have come to help us with our efforts. If you could each state your names,"

"Here?" Normalinda spoke up first.

"Yes, right here this is the whole team and instead of getting second hand information, we can just be up front with everyone right here,"

"No. Privacy please," Normalinda said.

"I think I would need at least two of my team members to be present don't you think even in privacy,"

"Sure, you pick," Normalinda said as she looked around the room and suddenly deemed the spokesperson of the group.

"Okay, Larisa and William come to the conference room,"

Larisa took nothing with her and followed into the conference room. William came into the conference room with his phone in his hand.

"Excuse me, your name is William?" Normalinda asked, looking William in the face.

"Yes," William replied.

"Why do you have your phone?"

"I don't go anywhere without it,"

"You will today. Please take it back to your desk," Normalinda replied.

"Okay," William said as he looked back at the Commander who quickly turned his head. Now, everyone was suspicious, especially Larisa.

"Until he returns, I'm Normalinda Martin and this is Xavier Martin, Duane and Annette Jackson along with Hank and Jasmine Simpson. We are the team that has been working to help resolve or at least slow down Train 606 but with little results," she explained.

No one moved or spoke but just nodded their heads in response and acknowledgement.

"Yes, I was told by my superiors that you have new technology that will help in the efforts even more, is that correct Ms. Jackson?" Commander said, directing his question to Annette Jackson.

Annette turned to Normalinda for her response. "That's Mrs. Jackson and what new technology are you referring to Commander?" Normalinda asked.

"We've been told that since the jewelry technology has been leaked, we have been wondering what is the next level of technology that you've discovered already or working on?"

"Yes, someone told the media mysteriously and unexpectedly. There seems to be a huge problem with leaks in this area, correct Commander?" Normalinda asked in a fashion more like a statement and accusation rather than a real question.

"Yes, we've been fighting them for years,"

"I see because it appears that there are ears everywhere in the region,"

"Also, correct,"

William returned quietly back into the conference room.

"Ms. Martin,"

"Mrs. Martin to you sir,"

"I'm sorry Mrs. Martin, what about the technology and our next steps,"

"My question to you Commander is what is the status of the warrants, etc."

"They have been requested but you know the judges have a full docket in Linkett and Lexington so it kind of slows down the process,"

"Exactly, slow enough so that the property is moved quickly, quietly and apparently because there are no warrants, they can move in plain site during the day time rather than at night which has been per usual,"

"Well, I see that you've been kept up to speed but what's the status of the technology though?"

"Right now, the same. Right, Mrs. Jackson?"

"Exactly, Mrs. Martin. The jewelry is always being worked so that it can be advanced to have a further radius and reach,"

"You sure that there is nothing else coming down your creative pipeline Mrs. Jackson?" Commander said.

"She just let you know that they are working on the current technology. Do you have any more questions for us today?"

"No, I think we've heard enough. Do you all need transportation since you came in the official cars?"

"We have transportation," Xavier Martin stepped forward and closer to his wife, Normalinda as he answered the question.

"Great. Larisa, would you mind escorting them out. William please stay," Commander asked.

"Sure," Larisa said as she grabbed the door to open it. She kept her eyes down so as to not make any eye contact with any of the visitors.

Once the door was closed behind her, she took the lead as they all walked toward the elevator, Duane Jackson suddenly said, "I'm hungry. Are you guys hungry?"

"Yeah, I'm starving,"

"Where should we go Officer Larisa to eat a great lunch? Do you have any suggestions?"

"What do you have a taste for?"

"A complete Smorgasbord,"

"Great, try the Taste of China which is new right down on Main Street,"

"Sounds good," Normalinda replied and held out her hand to Larisa and said, "Thank you."

"You're welcome," Larisa said in return and watched them all enter the elevator, turn around and give a slight nod in acknowledgement.

When Larisa returned to the conference room, she could hear Commander and William in a heated discussion.

"I don't like any of this. I am keeping up my end of the bargain, but by the way, why did you have your phone?"

"You know why,"

"This must stop. I can't do my job,"

"You must and you will do your job! Because the Amber alert will…" William suddenly stopped talking when he heard the door handle.

Larisa opened the door slightly while simultaneously knocking and stuck her head in and asked, "Commander, is there something that you need me to do next?"

"No, Larisa, we are good. I'll check in with you later to see what you thought of the meeting. Right now, I need to finish this with William,"

"Okay," Larisa said as she closed the door. Larisa knew that something huge was about to go down and it wasn't the regularly scheduled human trafficking.

Why had she suddenly just heard about an Amber alert too from LJ? Too many coincidences to be safe and not to be connected. Who was the Amber Alert for? Why would the Commander and someone in the LJ's law office be talking about an Amber Alert for someone that hadn't happened yet? As Larisa headed back to the office, she looked at the security monitors at the receptionist desk and noticed that the team that just left her had an automatic electronic car pull up to pick them up. No driver, once stopped, all doors opened and there was a brand-new license plate.

Larisa thought, 'Wow, come through again Dick Tracy.'

Safe House

As a child, Larisa loved all types of puzzles, solving word problems and reading mystery thriller stories. She would quiz Leena and LJ for answers and give them clues too. That's the main reason why they talked so much in code to this day. Therefore, it is also why solving clues and mysteries was the key to becoming a police officer and now an agent. In the academy, thy were taught to keep certain personal habits personal. Too much information gives people access and familiarity. Some things only you know and a few close friends. Well, unbeknownst to Commander or anyone else at headquarters, Larisa and Normalinda had been competitors and friends in the cheerleading arena for years through high school and college. After college, Normalinda went to law school and Larisa went to the academy.

Chinese was both of their favorite food and Main Street was always their code for house. Over the years, they had always kept in touch, no matter what. Normalinda's family lived and worked for many years on Xavier's family farm, the Miller Farm, where his father was a tyrant and corrupt business man, like his father before him. The Miller farm had been a major holding and sorting station for Train 606 for primarily forced labor until old man Miller died a few years earlier.

Xavier actually designed and built two of safe houses which were more like fortresses complete with the latest technology and ability to live months at a time without going into the outside world. There was one near Cincinnati and the other was now named the Martin farm which was mid-way between Lexington and Linkett. The super secure nature of the safe house made it perfect Xavier's domestic or international espionage consulting activity. When Xavier and

Normalinda took over the farm, they fired all of the employees and started all over from scratch making it a legal equine breeding and boarding operation. Xavier Martin had renamed the Miller Farm to the Martin Casa, Inc. which paid homage to Xavier's mother and both of their heritage. Larisa lived in a house with her family nearby. Do to the power and lucrative nature of the former Miller Farm, everyone knew but kept the farm's past secrets.

Unbeknownst to most, Larisa and Normalinda were extremely close friends who kept their friendship very secret and rarely were seen together in public. They were both cheerleaders, brought up totally different but remained friends over the years. Both of them worked in the legal, criminal justice field which was a surprise to them both.

At 5 p.m., Larisa received a text, 'Chinese was wonderful. See you on

Main Street at 6.' Larisa knew the sender and the instructions.

Hours later, Larisa pulled up to a huge one-mile gated drive way. You could not see the house from the street and there was no mailbox or speaker system at the gate. The massive two door black gate had a large gold M painted on each side in a beautiful script in the middle of the both sides of the gate. Larisa was only stopped for a few minutes and suddenly the gates opened. She drove the additional one mile to the circle drive way and there were two more humongous black front doors with the same gold M painted on the front.

Suddenly the front door opened, "Welcome to my humble abode," Xavier said with a large smile and quick hug.

"Humble my eye. 40,000 square feet is not a humble abode but a mansion," Larisa said as she entered the front door. She had come via her motorcycle and not either of her cars for safety reasons. She didn't even take the main roads, just cut through the fields and back roads for safety and time. Real country girls knew how to travel when necessary.

"Hey love, so good to see you," Normalinda said with a long lingering hug.

"You know everyone. Hank and Jasmine, Annette and Duane,"

"So great to see you guys again. By the way, Normalinda you gave Commander quite a run for his money today,"

"Yep, I did on purpose. He's dirty 'Risa,"

"I figured as much when he wanted everyone in the room to hear our conversation instead of in private and kept pressing about the now technology,"

"That part," Annette chimed in, "As you well know, I have been under attack and threatened for so long that it's not funny.

I have developed a tag just like you use for tagging breast cancer etc. for tracking people that's located inside of the body. I only have 1 client so far that has tried it and it was unusual because the person with the tag doesn't know that they even have it. It is easy to implant and not any more invasive than a shot."

"Genius, Duane I know that you are here to protect your wife, but I have to know, Hank and Jasmine, what is your role in all of this?"

"Moral support for Duane," Hank said.

"I'm moral support for Hank and mother for our twins. For all of our safety, I have to consult and work from home," Jasmine said.

"Because of this operation, we had to move, relocate and create a fortress just like Xavier," Hank explained.

"Friendship means everything to me. Hank is clearly my brother from another mother," Duane said.

"Wow this is rare," Larisa said.

"You telling me is beyond rare and something that I didn't grow up with because I was in military school, boarding schools, etc. Other students are NOT my friends for real. This has been a dream come true to have true friends and the love from Normalinda is a HUGE bonus," Xavier said.

"Exactly," Normalinda smiled.

"I'm a little jealous but I have my family too which works but it can get really lonely at night," Larisa admitted.

"I bet," Normalinda said.

"So, what's next?" Larisa asked.

"According to the inside, there is about to be an Amber Alert,"

"Oh, my goodness, even my brother heard about this Amber Alert,"

"It's going to be for somebody high profile,"

"Why the heads up and what do they want?"

"According to the inside, they want more than property. They want to shake down people on the inside for money so that the lower ranks can get rich just in case operations are shut down. Annette's invention could shut everything down so they want to be like bank robbers and do the stick 'em up and get the money like those in other countries do," Xavier explained.

"It's a world-wide problem," Normalinda said.

"So, we wait on the Amber Alert?" Larisa asked.

"Yes, because this might be our only way to at least capture someone and maybe get an agent or two out. The corruption has delayed any arrests, etc. so the inside believes that all of the property has been distributed and moved already but as far as getting any of the low-level soldiers, we don't have anything. This is the last act before they shut Train 606 down for this season,"

"They don't make enough on the property that they have?" Larisa asked.

"They do but it has to be shared for payoffs, etc." Xavier added.

"This is crazy!" Larisa exclaimed.

"So now we wait," Normalinda said.

"So now we wait," Larisa said quietly.

The rest of the night they continued catching up, remembering old times and eating Chinese food. It was a change of pace for Larisa to enjoy herself with others looking at pictures, old videos, etc. She was alone in this life and oftentimes felt lonely even with her family but at least for one night, she wasn't totally alone. When they said their goodbyes, she promised that she would text when she got home.

Next to the Last Piece of Property

Back in Linkett, Thursday night was for pre-game, pre-weekend partying in all of the nearby towns especially during football season. They couldn't wait until Friday to have a good time. It had been a big night at the country club and it was after 10:00 p.m. and although Janice was 18 years old, she still stayed to help clean up. The staff at the country club knew that they had only 1 hour and half to clean up and reset for the next day and then walk out of the building by 11:30 p.m. Definitely, too late for most anybody to be outside but definitely too late for a young pretty woman named Janice to be out this late waiting on a ride but that's what Alex had counted on. He had seen her before, told her that he would pick her up and she left her car at home. She fit the description of someone on his list. He had met her even in the grocery store on another day and made plans to meet her after work especially after Monday's train 606 meeting. She hadn't seen him in the meeting because she was forbidden because that was the only way an employee could keep their job. They had to set up, prepare and then leave. Alex pulled up to pick her up and when she got in the car they kissed and he put the sleep patch on her back. She was out in less than one minute.

Before Alex could pull off, the car stalled, and suddenly the back doors of the car opened.

"Why the hell are you back here?" It was the voice of the second Conductor. Alex couldn't see him because he had him in a chokehold around his throat and his head wouldn't move plastered against the headrest.

"Acquiring property. She's already out!" he was able to just whisper the words because he could hardly breathe.

"Boss you're right. She's out already," a soldier said.

Alex was coughing, rubbing his throat and trying to catch his breath from the tightness of the grip but said nothing.

"Better be a property out already. 'Cause remember we don't tolerate a weak link, just a dead one and we exterminate everyone. Also remember all cars and calls are tracked. Why did you pick her at the country club?"

"She fit the description on the requisition. I met her at the grocery store and followed her to work one day prior to the meeting to track her movements like y'all taught me. We haven't been dating, just talked a couple of times in the park. She didn't see me in the meeting at all,"

"Better not have. Alright we'll let you go this time but know that we are watching yo' ass closely," Second Conductor said.

They exited the car and Alex drove off to drop the girl to the holding station and to go about his business. He didn't have any time for drama or trouble. He had a job to do.

"He's got the package," the second Conductor said to a voice on the other line.

"Trap is set," the voice replied, "This property should keep the heat off of our backs because they'll be distracted because they have a high-profile person to look for. Good job!"

"Two for the price of one!" the second Conductor said.

The Last Piece of Property

The next day on the news morning show, the journalist said, "This is River Waters with a special announcement and Amber Alert for all citizens of the state to be on the lookout for Janice Baxter, daughter of Governor and Mrs. Baxter. She went missing on Thursday evening shortly after 9 p.m. There was security with her but when she went to the bathroom, she did not return for such a long time that security went into the bathroom and she was not there."

Larisa got the news and spat out her coffee. She had to get to headquarters as soon as possible to see what the next moves were.

Meanwhile at the Capitol, Governor Baxter didn't need the newscaster to tell him what was going. He was pacing the floor of the mansion trying to figure out why anyone would take his daughter. She had wanted to stay local, work a regular job and appear like a normal teenager when all along he and her mother knew that she wasn't normal. She was beautiful on the inside and out. She was so beautiful that it made people stare but especially men would stare for a long, lustful time.

"Where is she honey?"

"I have no idea dear,"

The head of security came into the house and the Governor shouted, "Where the hell is my daughter?"

"We don't know sir,"

"Don't know. Why don't you know?"

"She told us that she had a ride home from work. A new 'friend' and not to wait or follow her."

"And you listened?!"

"Sir, she has never given us an ounce of trouble before and the Country Club is highly secured with cameras,"

"I guess not last night,"

"What do you want us to do now?"

"Nothing, I'll handle it from here,"

"What does that mean sir?"

"You don't need to know. I am her father and the ultimate protector so since you can't protect, you're fired and I'll protect her myself. Get out!"

Suddenly the Governor's phone rang, "Hello! Where the hell is my daughter?"

"Well good morning to you too Governor. You'd think that you had spoken to someone at this number before," the voice with a wicked laugh.

"I have no need to play games today, what have you done with my daughter?" the Governor asked again more calmly. He realized that the voice on the other line didn't care about him or his daughter. They always wanted what they wanted and would go to any means to get it.

"Glad you calmed yourself down before this business of our turned really ugly. , For now, she is safe and definitely alright because we have some other business to tend to and then we'll give you the next instructions,"

"Give me instructions?!"

"I know that you are overly emotional right now or you wouldn't have made that statement because this our show and we are running it,"

"What's next?"

"You'll find out by tonight,"

"I better have my daughter back by late tonight,"

"Have you forgotten? You have no leverage, Governor. Just sit tight and wait on instructions,"

"Wait!" he yelled but the phone went dead.

The Governor knew that he was now out of his league and needed some help with this matter. He had let this go too far and with no security for his daughter or himself, he had to call in some help or he knew that his daughter could die.

Meanwhile, Annette, still at the safe house, was watching her tracking system indicator lights going crazy, answered her burner phone, "Hello."

"They have my daughter. Let's see how good your new tracking system is," the Governor said.

"I know, the system is going crazy because the device has been activated," Annette said.

"Great. They are supposed to call me back to let me know next steps," the Governor replied.

"Agree to all of their terms and hopefully, it will lead you either into a trap or directly to where she is. You can no longer trust your security. They are in on it. Xavier and his team will be your security from here and stay with you until the end of the process," Normalinda instructed.

"Great, go ahead and send them. I'll let you know when they call again," the Governor replied.

"It should be soon because everything seems to be moving very quickly,"

Both phones went dead and Annette relayed to Normalinda everything that the Governor had said.

"Okay, first team, head over to the Governor's mansion to be the body guards for the Governor," Normalinda said.

"What about Larisa?"

"I'll contact her and have her on standby to meet you all so that it can at least be legal,"

At headquarters, Larisa knew that something was not right all morning long. When she arrived earlier that morning, she tried the handle on Commander's office door but it was locked. She knocked and he only spoke to her through the door. He yelled for her to leave him alone and not come in unless he called for her. She asked if there were instructions and he said that there were none.

Most of the other officers were not in but out in the streets and William who was always in the building was nowhere to be found. was not in the building anywhere. Commander was locked in his office, the shades pulled and the door was locked.

's burner phone rang and it was Annette, "the tag has been activated. We are tracking it now."

"Okay, do you know where?"

"Yep, I'll send you the link,"

"Got it,"

"Be careful and know that Xavier, Duane and Hank are headed to the Governor's mansion to wait on further instructions. Once they know what the kidnappers want, we'll let you know. Do you have any officers that you trust to help you?"

"Not really. I'm on my own. I can't trust anyone in my department,"

"Well, you're in luck. Xavier called in his friends, special forces. They are 20 minutes away and will meet you at his safe house. I'll send you all of the information. Good luck," Normalinda said.

At Linkett High School, "The game is tonight and I'm so excited!" Melanie said.

"No, it's what is going to happen after the game that is the most important," Saundra said.

"You sure you don't want us to go with you?" Melanie asked and nearly pleaded.

"No, how would it look when I show up with 2 other people that were not invited,"

"What do we tell your parents if they ask where you are?

"Nothing because they are not going to ask. They are out of pocket tonight. Cindy, you haven't said anything? Saundra asked.

Cindy shook her head and turned her back.

"We'll keep each other company, won't we Cindy?"

Cindy just hunched her shoulders.

The game was going really good and the score was tied at 14.

"I'm headed to the bathroom. When are you leaving Saundra?" Cindy asked.

"When I get ready and don't you forget it,"

Melanie said, "That's not nice Saundra. When are you heading to the party?"

"Okay, I'll be nice this one time. After 3rd quarter, that's about when the time says on the invitation,"

"Okay," Cindy said as she walked off.

"Why are you so mean to Cindy?" Melanie asked.

"Just because. She'll never be me,"

"That doesn't make any sense. Of course, she will never be you because she's Cindy and you are Saundra,"

"Please stop talking Melanie,"

Melanie stopped talking and sipped on her iced Mocha.

When the score board indicated 4th Quarter, Saundra waved at Melanie and headed toward the house for the party nearby.

Saundra rang the doorbell. She heard no music or voices on the other side of the door but a very handsome guy opened the door and said, "Hey Beautiful! Let's link up!"

Saundra held out the invitation in her hand and said, "Hey, Bo why are you here? I got this invitation on my locker and I was told to come here for a party."

"Come on in, there is me, food and fun,"

When she stepped across the threshold, she saw Cindy.

"Cindy, how did you get in here?" Saundra asked, shocked.

"Wouldn't you like to know. Have fun and be good Saundra," Cindy replied and hugged Saundra as she placed the sleep patch on her shoulder. Bo caught Saundra just as she fell to the floor fast asleep.

"Thanks for your help, Cin. We'll see you next time," Conductor one said.

"Yes, we will," Cindy left out of the front door and headed back to the game with a smile on her face and purse filled with money.

Across town, the Commander's phone rang, "Hello."

"Commander, do you know where your daughter is?"

"Yes, she should be in her room sleeping because it is early Saturday morning,"

"Are you sure about that?"

"I'll call my wife,"

"Really? Are you sure that she is home too?"

"I haven't been home in 3 days because I am working both sides of this damn case. Tracking the 606 and helping you get that other property. I did what you asked, why did you take my family?"

"We had to ensure that you would do everything that we wanted done. The 606 is the best train and the most efficient. The last two properties were related. One for notification and the other for insurance. So, this is what we need you to do next?"

"I'm not doing nothing until you prove that you have them. Saundra, Mary!"

"They hear you but not for long if you don't follow instructions,"

"Or what?" Commander's phone went dead.

Meanwhile at Xavier's safe house, fortress. It was perfect for this operation.

Annette, Normalinda and Jasmine introduced the team to Larisa.

"Is this all? Four people?" Larisa asked.

"Girl, this is a special forces team and all that you need. They trained with Xavier. They can cover the four corners of any space and top sharp shooters at that. Alex sent us a message too that he is on the move with some bad assignment so be on the lookout for him to show up anywhere. Here is the location. Be careful. They are scheduled to make the trade at 6 p.m. tonight. Two million dollars for the Governor's daughter. The Governor has the money and everything."

The Commander's next call was to Larisa.

She let the phone ring twice because given all that had happened, she didn't know if she should answer the call or not. "Hello," Larisa said as she answered her personal cell phone.

"Help!"

"What's the matter Commander?"

"They have my daughter and my wife!"

"Who has your daughter and wife?"

"The bad guys,"

"Why would they want your daughter and wife?"

"I've helped them in the past. Now they want more and I don't want to do it,"

"After all of that the work I've been doing, you're why we've been tracking nothing! You have been helping them! You are just as dirty as them. No warrants, empty hotel rooms, empty warehouses for the past five years! What do you want from me?"

"It's my daughter and my wife,"

"All these years I thought you were serious about trying to help so many babies, girls and boys lost and now since it is your daughter and wife, I should help you? Someone who has been helping the bad guys all along. I trusted you! I believed you were for real. You are a fake, criminal cop! The money was so great that you turned your head to the many lives that have been traumatized and lost?"

"Listen Larisa, I'm desperate. They threatened me. They caught me and videotaped me,"

"You've been sleeping with kids?"

"No! She said that she was 18 but found out later that she was 16 and my daughter's friend, Cindy. I don't have any money so they are holding them for ransom. Either you help me or they'll kill my family and I'll…"

"You'll what?"

"I hate to say this but I know where your family lives and I'll take care of them too,"

"Is that a threat or a promise?"

"A promise because William is already there,"

"Hey Larisa," William said as Larisa didn't know that she was on three-way.

"William? Wow."

"Yep, look who is now in charge and got the top agent assignment," William said with a wicked chuckle.

"I promise you that if anything happens to my parents…" Larisa warned.

"It won't as long as you cooperate," William said.

"What do I need to do?"

"Come alone to the house," William said and hung up the phone.

Fortunately, Larisa was still at Xavier's safe house when the call came through. "What's going on?" Normalinda asked.

"They've got my parents! It's a whole kidnapping, holding for ransom thing going on. They didn't even tell me what they wanted just to come alone," Larisa said.

"That's a trap. They are planning to kill you and your parents. The team is going with you," Normalinda said.

"Thanks," Larisa said.

"You have to be done before 6 because we've got business across town with the Governor's daughter too,"

"Got it. Let's go!"

The team and Larisa all fit in her SUV and she gave them the coordinates and dropped them off about 1/4 mile from her house. She had both guns inside her socks as she headed toward the house.

Once she arrived, she got out of the car and yelled, "Mom, Dad!" Normally, she wouldn't have spoiled the element of surprise but she wanted her parents to know that she was there but William knew she was there too.

"Put your hands up," William yelled through the window. She did not hear any other voices coming from the house. After she got to the top step, the door opened and she could see not only her parents but her brother and sister all tied up in the middle of the living room.

"Surprise! The family is all here!" William yelled.

Larisa said nothing but kept her hands held high in the air. She quickly looked around the room and noticed that there were two other people in the room along with William. She recognized them both. Bo Rice, William's cousin and Alex, who Normalinda said might show up anywhere, here he was. She was proud of her family for not giving Alex away.

"William why is your little brother Bo here?"

"This is family business, didn't you know? I've hated you and your family since high school. Your dad caught me and Rob behind his barn that year. Shortly after that our parents were killed in a car wreck, Rob killed himself because he couldn't take it no longer and our lives were over! It's time for the Rice revenge!"

"You raped that girl and you were just 14. My dad saw you,"

"She asked for it and we aim to please,"

"You're despicable William and why did you drag Bo into it? He was just a baby when all of that went down,"

"After all of that publicity and loss, me and my brothers go the system. Rob and I got juvenile jail and Bo got foster care.

Torture, hunger and abandonment. Nobody wanted us but I cried and begged that judge to let Bo and I be together because that was all of the family I had left. No family came to rescue us and give us a better life. We were left to survive like animals and figure life out on our own. You got a perfect family with a mom, dad, brother and sister. Well, this will be sweet for me but I'm going to be able to do it all at one time, once and for all. Because not only have you been busy but your family has too so everyone must go," William said with a smirk.

"Shut up," the voice on the phone.

"Commander is that you?" Larisa recognized.

"Yes. I'm sorry Larisa, you are a fantastic agent but," Commander said sheepishly.

"But nothing, just shut-up!" Larisa yelled with a mixture of anger, fear and tears.

"We got her. She's mad, crying and everything Commander. You did a great job!" William said with a laugh.

"William, now you shut-up. This is hard enough for everyone but you and Bo have to do what you have to do to eliminate the evidence," Commander said.

"We will and good luck on getting your daughter and wife back," William said with a chuckle and wicked smile.

"What do you mean by that!" Commander yelled.

Suddenly two shots rang out. One for William and the other for Bo, but not Alex.

Commander was still on the phone, "So you did it already William? Bo what happened? Why only 2 shots? There are 6 people to eliminate?"

Larisa signaled her family to keep quiet and the only movement was the team coming into the house. One of the shooters pushed the end on the phone and it went dead. Alex helped Larisa untie her family, the team surveyed the damage and then, notified Normalinda who told them to get out of the house and they would do a further sweep and clean up later.

"Thanks for not giving me away," Alex said as he untied LJ.

"You're welcome," LJ said, "I would never have believed that you would be a criminal or a dirty cop, ever."

"I'm not but this has been the hardest job ever," Alex said.

"LJ, you and Leena know where to take mama and daddy until this is over. We'll debrief later on exactly how you guys got here, but it's over for now. I've got work to do," Larisa said.

"You both be careful," her mom said.

"Thank you, Risa and Alex. I'm so sorry but thankful for you and your friends, I guess. This is going to make me worry even more now," her dad said.

"I know daddy but you can tell that we've all grown up and can take care of ourselves and you too," Larisa said, "Now go!" Out the back door, her family went into the barn safe house.

Out the front door, Larisa, Alex and the team walked to their next assignment.

Alex turned to Larisa and said, "So, it was a set up for me too," Alex said.

"Yeah, it appears so, but why Bo?" Larisa asked.

"He was insider in the high school and young enough to set up the parties,"

"The parties?"

"You don't want to know,"

"I'll know more soon enough. Alex take my ATV to Xavier's and I'll meet you guys there later. It's clean,"

"Thanks," Alex replied.

"You, okay?" Larisa asked.

"No, but I will be. Thank you. I have had to stay focused but it has been great seeing you,"

"You too but don't have time for that right now,"

"True and hopefully, we can catch up after this mess is over," Alex said.

"Will it ever be over?" Larisa asked.

"Probably not but it is over for me. This type of undercover is NOT for me," Alex said.

"I get it and glad that you're safe. By the way, Commander thinks you're already dead. You'll be marked off the list, I guess so head to the safe house,"

"I'll be marked dead but always looking over my shoulder. Thanks for the ATV because the Conductor of Train 606 has all vehicles tracked. We'll leave it here as evidence for Xavier's team. We'll have to dispose of it all later,"

"Yeap, my parents' house will never be the same. Take care of you," Larisa replied.

"Be careful and take care of you too," Alex said as he turned the key on the ATV and headed toward the safe house. Mid-way there, he destroyed the phone, removed the tracking bracelet and breathed for the first time in a solid year. This mission had taken too much out of him. He had seen, heard and felt too much. The voices, screams and scenes would never leave his brain, heart or mind's eye. He would now become one of the consultants, background and support team, information providers to the new agents but always and more importantly, he would be a long-term client, customer or attendee on someone's therapy couch. Tracking humans is not only hard work for your body but too much strain on you mentally. The ability to maintain your own sanity amidst so much pain, torment and agony that is still thriving in the world. One day he really hoped to have some sense of normalcy and someone to share it with. For now, it was about recovery and safety.

While across town in his now empty home, Commander's phone rang again and a voice said, "Is it done?"

The Commander replied, "It's done. What about my wife and daughter?"

"Hold on. Don't be so anxious or you'll be picking them up in a body bag so don't push me. I still have the videos and you are not running nothing over here,"

"Got it. What's next?"

"River Port 7, Pier 6 at 6," the voice said and immediately the phone went dead.

Governor Baxter answered the phone and put it on speaker, "Hello,"

"You got the money?"

"Yep,"

"We've got your daughter,"

"Where and when?"

"Come alone to River Port 7, Pier 6 at 6."

Xavier texted the address to Normalinda who sent it to Larisa.

Half Rescue - Better than

It was 5:30 p.m. with 30 minutes to go but fortunately, they were only 5 minutes away from Pier 6. They were in plenty of time to set up surveillance to get off a shot if necessary. Xavier's team was in position already but Larisa's team, as they were now known, as the backup. The objective was to retrieve the Governor's daughter. Anything else would be a bonus. Larisa believes the Governor's daughter's kidnapping was a plant and decoy so that the other properties could get away and put all efforts on this rescue. This was another tactic to be added to Larisa's resource bank.

Larisa texted Normalinda, 'we're in position." Because of all of the advanced technology, tracking, etc., they had to use their own internal system to communicate. The traditional networks could not be trusted.

"Governor, get out of the car, put the money on the ground and put your hands up," a voice from the system loud speaker came for all to hear.

Governor Baxter did as he was told, got out of the driver's seat of a Black SUV with one large duffle bag which he dropped to the ground and he put his hands up.

The doors of the container were immediately opened and there stood Janice Baxter, the Governor's daughter, fully dressed and appeared from far away to be in good condition.

Suddenly, another SUV pulled up right next to the Governor's car. A man got out and it was Commander, "I'm here, where's my wife and daughter!"

"Commander, you don't have permission to speak and have been given no instructions. You are not in control here. Wait and we'll deal with you next. Janice you may go to your father,"

Janice immediately ran to her dad and was put in the back seat of the SUV. The Governor jumped in the SUV and they took off leaving the money on the ground.

Even though the Governor was gone, Larisa and her team did not leave and remained out of sight. Xavier's team followed the Governor's car back to the mansion.

Meanwhile at Pier 6, "Commander," the voice over the speaker said again, "Since you decided to interrupt, pick up the bag of money and open up the second container."

"Are they in there?"

"Just do as you're told,"

The Commander picked up the money, walked to the second container, opened up the door to find four FBI agents with guns drawn and the leader stating, "You're under arrest."

Governor and Mrs. Baxter received their daughter, Janice, which was their prize possession back home because of the advanced technology.

The Commander's life was over. His daughter and wife were nowhere to be found. He had been tricked once again but this time, he was tricked out of his family and career. A replacement would be assigned the next day and the cycle of corruption would begin all over again.

Epilogue

By 8:00 p.m. that same evening, Xavier and both teams of security were back at the Governor's mansion. They stood guard on the outside as well as inside the mansion, the Governor's daughter and wife were safely upstairs trying to bring some normalcy to the last few days events. Meanwhile in the Governor's office, Hank and Duane were observing while Xavier asked, "Governor, so you're as dirty as everyone else in this region."

"No, not really,"

"So why did they want your wife and daughter again?"

"I'm just turning my head and slowing down the process of being caught while getting funding for my re-election,"

"That's it. Re-election money or do they have something on you?"

"I'm bi-sexual,"

"Oh. I get it and like to do home videos too, I gather,"

The governor said nothing.

"Well, sir you are on your own. Hire your own security team. We need honesty here. I will not put my team, family, friends and others at risk for someone who is being a puppet. Your own your own. Goodbye. Let's go!" Xavier said as he quickly spun on his heals leaving the room with Duane and Hank while the Governor yelled, "Wait! Who is going to guard me and my family? Who is going keep us safe? You can't leave! No!!"

Once outside of the office, Xavier could still hear the Governor yelling 'come back!' but he radioed all of the team and said, "exit the mansion now!"

Minutes later, they all exited out the front door, climbed into their vehicles and left the mansion unsecured.

Thank You for Reading

Thank you for reading Tracked. This clearly is a topic, with a mission with NO clear conclusion.

When will it stop? When will it end? Never. As long as there are criminals willing to do anything for money to satisfy an appetite that seems insatiable at a price and cost that they can't seem to find a way to say no to. On the other end is a family out there who can't find the child, daughter or son that they lost to bring closure to a lifetime of trauma, pain and suffering that commenced because they turned their head, back or let their guard down for one minute too long. Snatched from a world they knew to a world that nobody deserves to know. Let the tracking continue and never stop until all are brought home alive or the bodies to be buried properly for closure.

Resources

National Human Trafficking Hotline

1-888-373-7888

https://www.safehouseproject.org/

https://survivorspace.org/trafficking

https://www.uscis.gov/humanitarian/victims-of-human-trafficking-and-other-crimes/

About the Author

Julia Royston/Kadance Royal (her pen name) is a retired librarian/educator, author, publisher, podcaster, and passionate writing coach. Her motto is, "Helping You Get Your Message to the Masses, Turn Your Words into Wealth and Be a Book Business Boss." Julia guides writers through every stage of the creative and publishing process.

As the author of over 145+ books and publisher of more than 400 titles, she brings unmatched expertise and encouragement to those ready to share their story. Julia has coached countless individuals to become published authors and successful entrepreneurs. She also leads five companies, a literary nonprofit organization and the editor of Book Business Boss Magazine.

To connect with Julia and begin your writing journey, visit www.juliaakroyston.com.

More Books by this Author